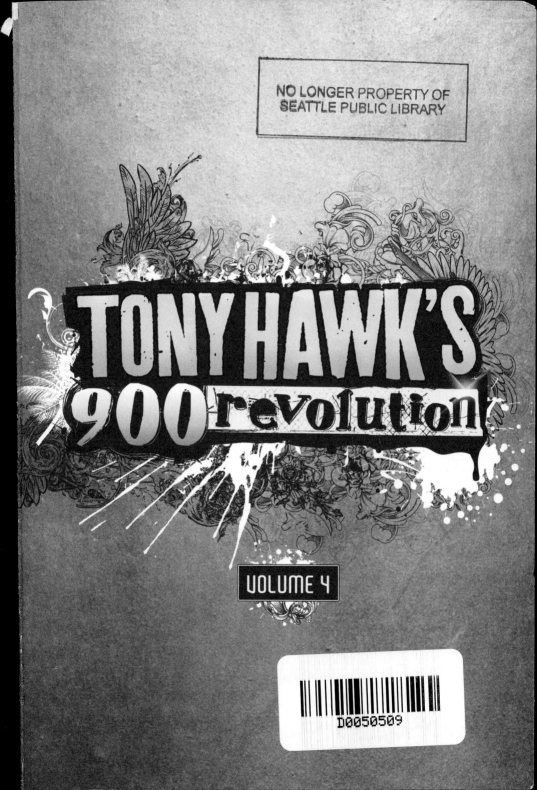

TONY HAWK'S
900 revolution

VOLUME 4

Tony Hawk's 900 Revolution
is published by Stone Arch Books
a Capstone imprint, 151 Good Counsel Drive, P.O. Box 669
Mankato, Minnesota 56002 www.capstonepub.com

Cataloging-in-Publication Data is available on the Library
of Congress website.
ISBN: 978-1-4342-3215-1 (library binding)
ISBN: 978-1-4342-3454-4 (paperback)

Summary: Joey Rail learned to ride before he could
walk. He's tried every two-wheeled sport imaginable,
but he's always come back to BMX freestyle. The skill,
patience, and power required for this daring sport suits
his personality. Joey is an outdoor enthusiast and loves
taking risks. But when he's approached by the first three
members of the Revolution, Joey must make a decision . . .
follow the same old path or take the road less traveled.

Photo and Vector Graphics Credits: Shutterstock.
Photo credit page 122, Bart Jones/Tony Hawk.
Photo credit page 123, Zachary Sherman
Flip Animation Illustrator: Thomas Emery
Colorist: Leonardo Ito

Art Director: Heather Kindseth
Cover and Interior Graphic Designer: Kay Fraser
Comic Insert Graphic Designer: Brann Garvey
Production Specialist: Michelle Biedscheid

Printed in the United States of America in Stevens Point,
Wisconsin.

092011
006366R

TONY HAWK'S 900 revolution

UNCHAINED

BY M. ZACHARY SHERMAN // ILLUSTRATED BY CAIO MAJADO

VOLUME 4

STONE ARCH BOOKS
a capstone imprint

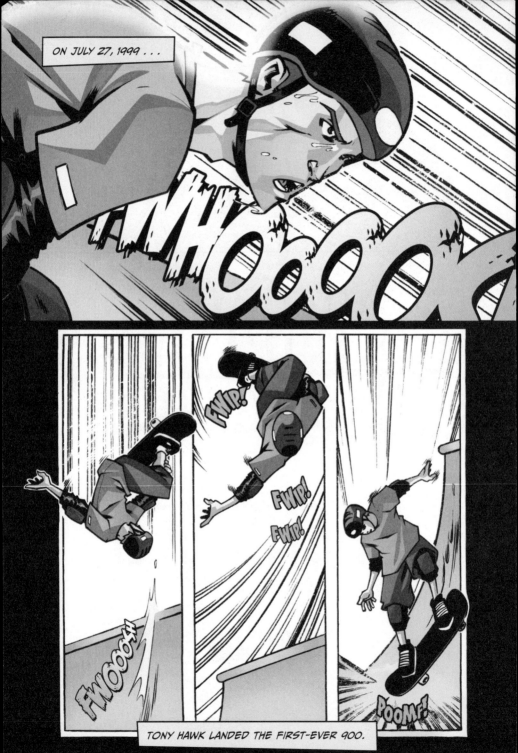

1

The storm was worse than anything Utah had ever seen. Sheets of rain flooded the red canyons from the Goblin Valley to the Canyonlands. Just outside the city of Moab, the entire Slick Rock terrain park was a maze of mud trails and rushing water. Dry creek beds had swelled to raging rivers, and Class II rapids churned like Niagara Falls.

High above these rushing water, fourteen-year-old Joey Rail clung to the roots of a hundred-year-old Ponderosa pine. Below him awaited certain death — a thousand-foot drop that no one could survive. Above him, on the edge of the rocky cliff, awaited a fate less certain but just as deadly: three members of the Collective were on the hunt . . . and Joey was their prey.

The members of the evil organization sloshed through thick mud, sweeping the area with their weapons, and pursuing Joey's tracks. Near the edge of the cliff, a stirring in the underbrush caught one of the teens' attention. Without hesitating, the boy spun with his weapon held to his shoulder and fired.

Pop! A tranquilizer dart blasted from his rifle and struck its target.

Suddenly, a massive black shape leaped from the underbrush and rushed straight for the Collective members. The beast stammered, grunted, and fell to the rocky ground as the tranquilizer took hold.

It wasn't human. And, more importantly, it wasn't Joey Rail.

"What is it?" asked one of the teens.

"A wild boar!" shouted another teen gleefully.

"Nice shot," said the third member with a snort, "but that's not the *pig* we're lookin' for."

"Well, I'm not taking any chances," replied the shooter. "That kid's already taken out two of our guys, and I'm not going to be next."

As the teens moved farther down the trail, Joey pressed a foot into the rock wall. He stood up and peeked over the lip of the cliff side. Trailing off into the deep recesses of the forest, the three teens disappeared.

When the Collective members were out of sight, Joey pulled himself back onto the main trail and took off running in the opposite direction. Silently, he angled his footfalls so they wouldn't make a sound. He mashed through puddles and pools of wet mud. Careful not to leave a trail, he bent tree limbs back, not breaking them, leaving no trace of his route.

Then Joey zagged right and headed deeper in the forest, away from the cliffs, the rushing river, and jagged rocks below.

As he cut through the forest, he ran the current situation through his mind. This day had started like any other, but now he was struggling to make sense of the strangeness that had swallowed him up . . .

2

It was raining. Hard. In the Southwest, a good downpour could close roads, schools, and businesses. But a little rain wasn't going to stop Joey Rail. His BMX gear had been packed for weeks — nothing would keep him from entering his first racing competition.

Like most kids growing up in Moab, Joey learned to ride before he could walk. He'd tried every two-wheeled sport imaginable — motocross, mountain biking, you name it — but he always came back to BMX freestyle. The patience and power required for the sport suited his personality. Unfortunately, in Utah, *racing* was king. Although he'd perfected nearly every freestyle trick imaginable, Joey always wondered if his street skills would translate to the dirt track.

Only one way to find out, thought Joey. He stood inside his dad's rusted out shed, checking the chain on his custom-built bike for the hundredth time.

"Maybe it'll be canceled," said a voice from behind.

Joey looked up to see his mother standing in the doorway. She was holding a small lunch cooler.

"Not this race, Mom," said Joey. He walked over to her and took the packed lunch from her hands. "Once we're up on that mountain, there's only one way down." Joey reached back and patted the seat of his BMX bike. "Rain or shine."

"You'll do great," said his mom. "Don't be nervous."

"I'm not," Joey replied. He gave a crooked smile, and then bent down and shoved the lunch cooler into his large green rucksack. It was his father's pack, with RAIL embroidered on the side.

Joey's mother reached out and ruffled her fingers through her son's hair. "He's very proud of you, you know?" she said.

Master Sergeant Tim Rail had been deployed to Afghanistan seven months earlier. His absence was just now starting to affect Joey. He knew his father had an important duty — to protect him and protect the country's freedom — but sometimes none of that seemed to matter. Joey simply wanted his father home.

"I just wish he was here," said Joey.

"So does he, dear. Trust me," replied his mother. "But he'd tell you to forget about the sponsors, the rain, all of that stuff — just ride your best and everything will work out."

Joey nodded. "I just don't want to let him down," he said.

"Never," his mom said. "You're a Rail, right? No matter what happens, you'll survive."

Joey's mom picked up her son's helmet and held it in her hands. A bird's feathered head had been airbrushed on the surface. It was a brown and black Rail bird. The clear coat of paint was scuffed and dented from where Joey bailed on a vert ramp last year, but otherwise it was in pretty good shape.

His mother knew how dangerous BMX could be. Joey had suffered broken bones, sprained joints, and too many cuts and bruises to count. But his mother knew something else: like his father, Joey was a survivor.

Before he left for Afghanistan, Joey's dad had spent every summer in the wilderness camping, hunting, and fishing with his son. Tim came from a long line of outdoorsmen. He felt obligated, and proud, to pass on some basic survival skills to Joey, just in case he would ever need them.

Joey twisted a small, cobra-braided bracelet made from a parachute cord on his wrist. His father gave him the crude gift on their last camping trip. It wasn't much, but it reminded Joey of his father's creativity and ingenuity — traits Joey always tried to keep in mind while riding his BMX bike.

"You'll kick butt out there," his mother added with a smile. She placed a finger under her son's chin and pushed his head up to meet her gaze. "Now, are you sure you don't want me to come watch?"

"You can't," answered Joey. "I know how busy you are at the hospital."

She handed the bike helmet back to her son. "Be sure to wear this. I don't need things to get any busier in the ER."

"Don't worry," said Joey.

The sound of a truck horn blaring the opening notes to "La Cucaracha" echoed from outside.

Joey's mother rolled her eyes and frowned. "Tell that boy to change that horn," she groaned. "It sounds like a lunch wagon, for crying out loud!"

Joey laughed. He picked up his bag, locked his helmet onto his elbow, and hoisted his bike onto his shoulder. "Will do," he said, heading out of the garage. "See you later, Mom."

* * *

Outside, a black 4x4 truck gurgled and sputtered in the driveway. In the cab, Joey's friends waited for him.

"We're gonna be late," grumbled Derek, looking down at his watch and laying on the horn.

"We're okay," Wendy said. She sat in the passenger seat, eating a breakfast burrito. "As long as you don't drive like you ride . . ."

"What's that supposed to mean?" asked Derek.

"It means —" Wendy started, but the sound of rubber tires on metal made her stop. She looked back to see Joey dumping his BMX bike and gear into the bed of the pickup.

"What Wendy means to say, Derek," said Joey, sliding in the passenger-side door, smooshing Wendy into the center of the seat, "is step on it!"

Without hesitating, Derek popped the emergency brake and threw the truck into drive. They were off on what Joey hoped would be the adventure of a lifetime.

"Here," said Wendy. She handed Joey a warm, greasy bag of food. "We got you some road munchies."

Joey opened the bag, pulled out a handful of fast food hash browns, and took a bite. Grease slipped down Joey's cheek as he bit into the potato patty.

"Blech!" said Derek, looking over at his friend. "How can you eat that garbage?"

Joey wiped his chin with the back of his hand and held the hash brown out to Derek. "Sure you don't want any?" he said, smiling.

Derek gagged. "Seriously, bro, I think I'm going to be sick," he said, covering his mouth.

"It's my lucky breakfast!" Joey exclaimed. "Fried egg and cheese on a muffin, hash browns, and —"

"A vomit bag?" Derek interrupted.

"Very funny," said Joey. Out of his pack, he pulled his multi-tool utility knife from its leather sheath and flipped open the blade. Carefully, Joey cut the breakfast muffin in two equal parts, wrapped up one of the halves in a napkin, and placed it back in the bag.

"Don't tell me Derek actually changed your mind about breakfast," said Wendy.

"Nope," said Joey. "Just saving it."

"For what?" asked Derek.

"My victory lunch, of course," replied Joey. He savored one final bite and wiped off his mouth. "Every time my dad and I went camping, we'd get this breakfast as we left civilization. Sort of a last meal — you know, before we started 'living off the land.' Eating berries, grubs, bugs, and stuff like that."

"Ew!" Wendy exclaimed. "Remind me never to go camping with you and your dad."

"Speaking of him," Derek chimed in. "When's he due back, anyway?"

Joey got quiet as he looked out at the passing scenery. "His tour in Afghanistan was extended another three months," he said.

Wendy rubbed a hand on her friend's shoulder. "Sorry, man," she said.

"At least he's good at his job, right?" Derek added.

Joey nodded and then leaned back in the seat and shut his eyes. "Wake me when we get there, okay?" he said, letting out a little yawn.

"I told you, you shouldn't have eaten that garbage," Derek shot back.

"Yeah, I guess you were right, man," replied Joey. Then he drifted off to sleep, wishing a stomach ache was the only source of his uneasiness.

3

An hour later, Joey woke up. They had finally arrived at Slick Rock, a 300-acre terrain park covered with hazardous trails, jumps, vert ramps, mud holes, rails, and hundred-foot cliffs. *Paradise*, Joey thought.

As the truck slowly entered the parking lot, Derek whistled at the amount of people who were already there, gearing up and getting ready for the race. Most competitors had gotten there super early to set up their "base camp" in the parking lot.

Only twelve feet wide at its largest point, the trail was solid mud. With the nonstop rain, visibility on the trails would be pretty bad, and the creek beds would be overflowing with water. Loose rocks would make slipping off the edge of the cliff a real possibility.

Vinyl banners of every size and color, sporting logos from various bike manufacturers, and energy drinks were tied to makeshift posts and metal pipes. The sponsor of the race — and the one putting up the five thousand dollar prize money — was Spaz Cola.

"That stuff is nasty," said Derek, stepping out of the pickup and spotting the Spaz Cola banner. "Not to mention that it's just a bottle of high fructose corn syrup and green dye."

"At least their paychecks clear," said Joey, having won several of their freestyle competitions in the past.

"And you'd certainly know about that, kid!" a voice rumbled out from behind him.

Joey turned and spotted Robert Stevenson, the owner and operator of Spaz Cola. He was a thin man, about six feet tall with a gaunt face and a beak-like nose.

"Mr. Stevenson," Joey said.

"I wasn't sure if you'd show up," Stevenson said, adjusting his umbrella. "Since the weather's so bad."

"Wouldn't miss it, sir," Joey said.

"Lots of major sponsors are out here, Joey," Stevenson added. "A perfect opportunity to show 'em what you can do on a dirt track, huh?"

"I'm just here to ride, sir," replied Joey. "Maybe have a little fun while I'm at it."

"Ha!" Stevenson laughed. "That's why I've always liked you, kid. You're here for the ride, not the money."

Joey smiled. "The money's not half bad either."

Stevenson tilted his head back and let out a belly laugh. "Very true!" he exclaimed. "But seriously, Joey, now that you're riding the dirt, when can I get you on my crew? We all think you'd be a great addition to the Spaz Cola team."

"I'm sorry, sir, but —" Joey began.

Holding up a silencing hand, Stevenson smiled and nodded his head. "I thought you were serious about the money not being a concern," he said. "But if you need more, I'm willing to pay it."

Joey reached into the truck and opened his rucksack. He starting pulling out his old protective gear and strapping it onto his legs and forearms. "I wasn't lying, sir," said Joey. "Actually, it's just the opposite." Joey pointed up the mountain at the Spaz Cola team. Each teen had a brand-new bike and the latest gear. "Those kids just ride for the green. No offense. I understand their motivations, but I hope you understand mine."

"Someone raised you right, kid," Stevenson said, jabbing Joey in the shoulder. "But, if you ever change your mind, we'll be here."

"Thank you, sir," Joey said.

"Oh, and good luck today, son," Stevenson added as he began walking away. "Although I'm hoping to keep a little of that prize money for myself."

"Thank you, sir," said Joey.

"Well, that was completely awkward," said Derek once Stevenson had disappeared from sight.

"Totally," replied Joey with a smirk.

"That's a lot of money to just walk away from," Wendy added. "I'm proud of you, Joey."

"Yeah, I know," said Joey. "But my dad would never let me take it. Not before going to college, anyway. Besides —" Joey pulled a Kevlar-plated armored vest over his head and buckled the sides. "— like we always say, 'The ride's the most important thing.' If the winnings help me pay for school, then great. But I don't want to compromise in getting there."

"Okay, Gramps," Derek joked as he pulled the BMX bike out of the truck.

"Shut it," Joey said with a laugh.

"Ahem!" interrupted Wendy. "Could we get back to business, guys?" She pulled out a map of the racecourse and pointed to the path that led up the mountain. "Basically, this race is a free-for-all. Ride to the summit and return to the finish line as quickly a possible."

"What?" asked Derek, puzzled. "No markers?"

"Why do you think I picked this race?" asked Joey. "How each rider gets up and down the mountain is up to them. It's perfect for a freestyler like me."

Joey eyed the map closely. He was confident in his abilities on a bike, but he knew that Slick Rock Mountain was a dangerous place. Loose rocks, narrow trails, and sheer cliffs meant life-or-death decisions at every turn.

"Piece of cake," Joey finally said, not wanting to show an ounce of fear. His father wouldn't have. "Come on. Let's get the rest of the gear unpacked. The race is about to begin."

* * *

The metal starting gates were ready, and all nine riders were lined up in their slots. Like bulls at a rodeo, each of the riders bucked and moved. Each tried to get the best foothold on their pedals, kicking off the mud stuck deep in their boot treads.

Joey had wanted slot number one. That position had a nice downward slope to the right of the chute, and the position would've given him an early boost of speed. Unfortunately, Stevenson had placed Joey in position number five, right in the center of the pack.

Derek had protested, but Joey didn't mind the slot once he was in position. In fact, he kind of liked it. The difficult position gave him an opportunity to challenge himself — and he always welcomed a challenge.

Clicking the safety strap on his helmet, Joey waited patiently for the race to begin. The start of any competition — any ride — always had an instant calming effect on him. He knew most riders' hearts were pounding through their chests. But for him, this was the easy part.

Finishing? thought Joey. *That's another story altogether.*

With the flick of the official's wrist, the green flag went up. Eight teenagers tensed their leg muscles as they rose from their seats in a poised position. The only sound was the soft patter of raindrops against bike helmets.

In a blur of emerald cloth, the flag dropped.

With a loud clang, the gate opened.

Riders pushed with all their might against their pedals. The race was on.

Joey burst from the gate. He pedaled hard and took the lead right away. The first turn was coming up. Joey knew it was an important one.

Luckily, his friend Derek had spent the night deciding the best setup for his bike. He knew that because of the rain conditions, traction would be terrible. Knobby tires, stiff downhill forks, and a good composite frame often meant the difference between winning and losing. But on this course, in this weather, it meant the difference between life and death.

Joey powered into the first turn, whipping mud from his rear tire. Hot on his heels was one of the Spaz Cola riders.

Joey smiled. He shifted into high gear and settled onto the course. It was way too early to be worrying about trailers now.

A series of four rollers were coming up. Joey was ready for them. He took pressure off his knees and made them into shock absorbent springs.

One after another, the small moguls came. Joey found it faster to peddle through them rather than jump over them. As small as they were, they were soft and moist. The harder the impact, the slower he went.

Joey heard another rider struggling just behind him. Peaking over his shoulder, he grinned slightly as he saw the Spaz teammate pop his front tire down too hard, getting it stuck in the mud. The riders behind him frantically adjusted their directions as they twisted and turned, trying not to crash into the downed rider.

As Joey hit the straightaway, the rest of the pack was two bike lengths behind. He rocketed into the forest, hunkered down, shifted his weight back, and poured on the speed. With that, Joey was out of sight.

Derek watched the excitement from the stands. "There he goes!" he shouted. "How long we got?"

"About one hour till they come back," replied Wendy.

"Whoa!" Derek exclaimed.

Funny enough, Joey was thinking the same thing as he came up to a tabletop and flew off. Most BMX freestyle competitions were five minutes, max. This BMX race was going to test more than Joey's skills. It would test his endurance as well.

Fortunately, even the most experienced racers today hadn't ridden this type of track before. This was a new freestyle, cross-country BMX race where the riders chose their own paths. The winner was the first one down the mountain in the shortest amount of time. Simple. Joey had one advantage: thanks to those camping trips with his father, he knew Slick Rock better than most.

As Joey came out of the third turn, he breezed quickly through the rhythm section of the course. The last part of the track was coming up — the cross-country section.

Just then, Joey noticed a jump going left toward a steep climb up the mountain. The ascent would be a tough one — it would take him farther into the forest than he would have liked. On the other side of the shortcut, it was almost a straight shot downhill to the base of the mountain and back to the finish line. He knew that the other riders would never attempt the risky shortcut.

But, with nothing to lose, Joey was willing to try.

Grinning, Joey busted left, turned quickly, and popped up the jump. He sailed over a downed tree and onto the single track, heading up the mountain and away from the rest of the pack.

The falling rain shielded him from the other riders like a curtain. Joey was on his own — and that was just how he liked it.

5

Joey pedaled the steep incline of the mountainside. On his left was the downhill slope leading back to the starting line and the regular BMX speed track. He glanced down, trying to gauge how far above the small crowd of onlookers he was riding.

Joey didn't like crowds. He enjoyed the solitude of the ride. Man, machine, and the elements. It was him against himself — and against the clock.

The teen took a deep, controlled breath, attempting to lower his heart rate. At this altitude, the air was thin, and Joey was feeling light-headed. He knew the best thing to do was relax. At this angle, five hundred more feet and he'd reach the summit. Then, after a sprint through the woods, he'd be crossing the finish line.

Joey looked right and wished he hadn't. A sheer, five hundred foot cliff bottomed out into a river. One slip on the single-track trail, and Joey Rail would be dead.

Maintaining a safer pace, nearly twenty minutes passed before Joey reached the summit. However, he knew he'd made the right choice. *Probably took ten minutes off my overall time*, he thought.

Joey paused a second to get his bearings. He reached into his pocket and pulled out his copy of the terrain map. He checked his position, traced a line to the finish with his finger, and then looked up ahead.

He would have to cross the creek about half a mile down and, if he were lucky, the bridge would still be there. The real danger, however, came after that — the descent. In the back of his mind, Joey knew that summiting a mountain was the easy part. But, as his father had warned, accidents happen on the way *down*.

Joey wiped the rain from his safety goggles. With any luck, the continuing downpour would let up before the grueling descent. However, Joey's dad had taught him something else: "When it comes to luck," he always said, "you make your own."

Joey folded the map and shoved it back into his pocket, then took off down the hill. Joey would take charge of his own destiny.

* * *

A short while later, Joey traveled back and forth down a steep, switchback trail. The rainfall had turned the packed dirt to soft mud. Luckily, Joey's tires were still able to grip the path.

Just then, Joey spotted a strange tire track in the trail. He stopped suddenly, grinding his rear wheel into the mud. Sniffing up at the air, Joey was sure he smelled smoke — not from campfire, but from engine oil or fuel. It was a distinct smell, and one distinctly out of place on this backcountry trail. Something was wrong.

Joey dismounted his bike and walked over to the edge of the cliff. Fifty feet below him on the twisting trail, a small motocross bike lay mangled and smoking. The teen rider was trapped beneath it, his right leg pinned under the mass of crumpled metal.

Studying the scene, Joey spotted fuel leaking from the gas tank. It combined with the oil that dripped steadily from the engine. The deadly soup was smoking and burning in a fire crackling near the bike's manifold. If the winds weren't blowing and the rain hadn't been falling, the bike would have gone up like a barrel of dynamite, and the mystery rider would already be dead by now.

What should I do? Joey wondered.

The teen knew he didn't have time to go back for help. A single spark could set the bike ablaze at any second. Joey couldn't let the rider die.

Joey untied the ends of his bracelet and removed the braided parachute cord from his wrist. Twisted and unwrapped, the bracelet was actually a survival tool — another one of his father's brilliant inventions. The bracelet uncoiled into a thin fifty-foot cord, which had the tensile strength of three hundred pounds.

Joey quickly secured one end of the cord to a nearby tree. He threw the other end down the side of the cliff. Then, wrapping his leg around the cord for support, Joey slowly lowered himself down to the plateau below.

At the bottom, Joey moved quickly to the rider's side. "Hey, pal," he said. "Can you hear me?"

Joey glanced over his left shoulder and saw the fuel tank. Kicking mud with his boot, he was able to divert the fuel flow away from the fire, giving him a few more precious moments.

The rider groaned. "W-what happened?"

"Looks like you missed a turn, pal," said Joey, trying to keep the rider calm. "Come on. We've got to move you." Joey reached down with both hands and scooped up the motocross bike's rear tire in his gloved palms.

"When I lift," said Joey. "I need you to slide your leg out, okay?"

The helmeted rider nodded nervously.

Then, with a sudden burst of adrenaline, Joey lifted the bike's tire off the ground. The mysterious rider quickly pulled his injured leg free from the wreckage.

"Thanks," said the young man.

"Don't thank me yet," Joey replied. He crouched down and threw the rider over his shoulders in a fireman's carry. "Just hold on."

Joey quickly moved back to the dangling parachute cord. He wrapped one foot around the cord and grabbed on tight with his gloves. Then, like a professional free climber, Joey moved hand-over-hand up the rocky cliff. Although Joey had never climbed with someone on his back, he usually traveled with a heavy backpack, and this wasn't all that different. Besides, Joey knew he didn't have any other choice.

Gas from the motocross bike spilled over the small mud dam he had created. Soon, they'd both be toast. Inches at a time, and with the heavy weight of the injured motorcyclist on his shoulders, Joey ascended the cliff.

Ten feet from the top of the cliff, Joey felt flames lick at his heels. The engine had ignited.

Joey moved faster. Shifting his weight, he squatted down and launched up with his legs, pressing on the top of his foot. The man bounced up and rolled from Joey's shoulders, landing on the top of the cliff, away from the edge.

Flames shot skyward. The sound of a high-pitched spark rang out. *KA-BOOOM!* The motorcycle exploded in a massive ball of flame.

Joey dug his fingers into the soft mud and flipped himself up and over the cliff ledge, landing on his back. As he rolled himself over, he felt fragments of metal and plastic sail by him.

Joey gasped for air. Hot, moist vapor exhaled from his mouth. The strain of climbing was bad enough, but the additional weight had completely drained him.

"Thank you," said the rider through the fogged up lens of his motocross helmet.

Joey could barely move. He nodded and waved at him. "No worries, pal," he said, still struggling to breath. "Just glad I smelled the smoke."

Reaching up, the cyclist removed his helmet. The boy was hurting, and it showed on his young face as his blue eyes gazed up painfully at Joey. His hair was wet from sweat and matted to his head, but Joey immediately recognized him.

"Aren't you Omar Grebes?" asked Joey.

Omar nodded and smiled painfully. He dropped his helmet to the ground and leaned back against the trunk of a nearby tree. "You know me?" he said.

Joey rose to his knees. "Who doesn't?" he replied. "You're the captain of the Revolution team, right? I just read an article about you guys the other day. Your team has some of the top competitors in, like, every action sport imaginable. I can't believe I'm actually meeting one of you!"

"A dream come true, right?" said Omar, clutching at his injured leg.

"No, of course not," Joey replied, realizing the situation they were both in. "I just meant —"

"BMX racing, huh?" interrupted Omar. He pointed at Joey's bike on the nearby path.

"Yeah," Joey replied. "Well, actually I prefer to ride freestyle, but today is an exception."

"I thought so," said Omar.

"What do you mean?" asked Joey, puzzled.

"You're Joey Rail, correct?" Omar replied.

Joey's eyes went wide with shock. "How did you — I mean, why do you know my name?"

"I know a lot more than that," said Omar. "But I'll explain everything later."

"What were you doing out here?" Joey asked.

"Getting hurt, obviously," grumbled Omar. He winced and grabbed his injured leg.

Joey moved toward the teen. He leaned down and cradled Omar's right foot in his hands. Slowly, Joey slid his fingers over his ankle, checking it for a break.

"Does this hurt?" Joey asked.

Omar shook his head.

Joey positioned his hand on a different spot. "How about here?" he asked, squeezing gently.

"Ah!" Omar yelped in pain. "Stop! Stop!"

"Well, good news," said Joey. "It's not broken, and your Achilles tendon is still intact."

"And the bad news?" asked Omar.

"This is the worst sprain I've ever seen," Joey said.

"And how do you know all this?" Omar asked.

"My mom's a nurse, and my dad's an Air Force paratrooper," Joey explained. "Oh, and I've been in the hospital a couple of times myself."

Joey rose. He pulled a utility knife from his pocket, snapping opening the small saw-toothed blade. "I'm going to find some flat pieces of wood," he said.

"What for?" asked Omar.

"A splint," answered Joey. "You'll be able to walk, but you won't be hittin' the halfpipe anytime soon."

Joey began sawing off a downed tree limb with the tiny blade. Soon, he had trimmed two sticks to the length of Omar's leg. Finally, Joey stopped and turned to the injured skater. His eyes narrowed.

"So you gonna tell me?" Joey asked, placing the sticks near Omar's feet and kneeling beside him.

"Tell you what?" asked Omar.

"Why I found a world-renowned skateboarding champion half dead on the side of Slick Rock Mountain," said Joey.

"Oh, that," said Omar.

"Yeah, *that*," Joey shot back. He stared Omar in the eyes, hoping to determine if the boy was preparing to lie or not.

Omar simply looked away, avoiding the question.

"Fine," said Joey. "If you're going to make this difficult, then so am I."

Joey put his head down and began to splint Omar's right ankle. First, he removed the teen's leather boot and his sock. Then, Joey snapped open his utility knife again. He sliced the sock into long strips, which he used to tie the two sticks around Omar's ankle.

"Too tight?" asked Joey, securing the knotted socks.

"Ah! Yeah, man," Omar exclaimed, "I can barely feel my toes!"

"Perfect," said Joey with a smile. "Now try to stand."

Omar struggled to his feet. "Nice," he said. "I owe you." The teen placed a bit more weight on his injured leg, but a sharp pain shot up his calf. He stumbled.

Joey grabbed Omar's arm, preventing him from falling. "Okay, calm down, champ," said Joey. "You're going to have to take it easy for a while, okay?"

"No can do, man," said Omar, steadying himself once again. "I gotta go."

"Where?" asked Joey. "I mean, at least let me go get you some help —"

"No!" Omar snapped.

Joey Rail looked at his surroundings. Though the rain had washed away much of the evidence, he still got a pretty clear picture of what had happened. Broken tree limbs, several sets of footprints, tire skid-marks from Omar's BMX bike leading to the edge of the cliff.

Omar Grebes was in trouble.

"How many are there?" Joey asked quietly.

"What?" Omar asked.

"It looks like about five people were chasing you on foot, and got the drop on you here," replied Joey. He pointed at a nearby section of wet ground where the footprints were deepest.

"Then they forced you to swerve," Joey continued, "and that's when your bike went airborne."

Omar grinned. "You're not going to believe me —" he began.

"Try me," interrupted Joey.

"Fine, but we have to move," Omar said, starting to hobble away.

"Dude, the way down is over here," said Joey.

"Yes, but I'm going *up*," replied Omar.

They trekked toward the plateau of the mountain. It was the exact opposite direction of civilization and the medical attention Omar needed.

"Why?" asked Joey. "Tell me what's going on!"

"The Revolution isn't just a sports team," Omar started. And for the next fifteen minutes, he told Joey the story of the team, their origins, and their purpose. He explained to him about the Artifacts, the Keys, and the other sect — the Collective — who fought them for control of the Fragments.

Joey listened as they continued along the muddy path. He could barely believe the tales of supernatural energies, global conspiracies, and international adventure.

As they reached the end of the man-made trail, Joey turned to Omar. "So what are you doing out here?"

"Still searching," Omar said.

Omar reached into a pocket and removed a handheld GPS receiver. Its crosshairs locked in on the North American continent, then zoomed in within three miles of their location: the crest of the summit.

"No way you're climbing, bro," exclaimed Joey.

"Why did this have to happen now?!" cried Omar as he looked around. "Why couldn't I have landed in Baja or Hawaii or somewhere?"

Joey could sense the urgency in Omar's voice. He had to find a way to help. "How much of a head start do these 'Collective' guys have on you?" asked Joey.

"Dunno," replied Omar. "Thirty minutes, maybe?"

"Okay, and I assume they're using trail maps to navigate the area. Satellite maps, at best," said Joey, thinking out loud.

"Probably," Omar said.

Joey turned his face to the sky. The rain was now coming down in sheets. He knew that there wasn't any way Omar could make it to the summit on a bum ankle.

Joey looked east. He eyed the trails, which twisted and turned up the to crest of the far mountain. About five miles total. *Thirty minutes on a good day,* Joey thought. "I'll have to book it," he said out loud.

"What?" said Omar.

"Look, man, why don't I just go in your place?"
Joey replied. "I know the terrain. Trust me, I can get
up there and back before those dudes *and* get that
Fragment first. You head back down the mountain. I've
got some friends down there named Derek and Wendy
— they'll help you out. When I've got this Fragment
thing, I'll bring it right to you."

"No way, man," Omar exclaimed. "I can't ask you to
do that."

"You didn't," said Joey. "I'm offering."

"Look," Omar began, wiping the rain from his
brow. "I didn't want to tell you this, but these guys are
packing some serious hardware."

"You mean, guns?" Joey asked.

"No, but just about everything else," answered
Omar. "Tranquilizer darts, taser batons, capture nets,
and worse."

"Are they on some kind of safari hunt?" Joey joked.

"You could say that," Omar replied, looking totally
serious. "These guys mean business, man. I can't let you
go. It's my duty —"

Omar took one step forward. Once again, pain
radiated through his entire body. He collapsed to the
ground, tried to stand up but just fell over again. Omar
didn't seem capable of admitting defeat.

Joey crossed his arms over his chest. He glared down at Omar, who was now covered from head to toe in mud. "How about now?" Joey asked. "Still think you can do this without me?"

Omar spit, and then slowly shook his head from side to side.

"Fine," Joey said. "So where are we going?"

6

By midday, most of the paths up the mountain had turned into ruts. As precious few minutes remained, Joey Rail pedaled through the water and the mud. Soon, he stopped, leaned against a Ponderosa pine, unbuckled his Kevlar vest, and removed the heavy padding from inside. The less weight he carried, the faster he could travel. Tight now, speed was his number one priority. His second: reach Omar's coordinates before the Collective members could get their hands on the Fragment. Whatever *that* was.

Omar's GPS device was attached to his hip. A blinking red dot marked his exact location on a digital map. Joey knew this area well, but he'd take all the help he could get at this point.

Taking a second look at the GPS, Joey figured he'd cut across the northeast side of the mountain. If he forded the main river and climbed the east face, he'd get to the location fifteen minutes before the Collective. That would be more than enough time to find the Fragment and move out undetected.

But Joey knew he had to be careful. He didn't want to end up like Omar had, bruised, broken, and alone on the side of a mountain. There was no one else up here to rescue him.

* * *

Meanwhile, another race continued on the mountain. The first BMX riders from that morning's competition emerged from the forest trail. They flew over a jump and landed hard into the marked course. As riders neared the finish line, a crowd of onlookers gathered to see who had gotten there first.

One by one, the riders pushed into the final turn. With only a hundred yards to go, the captain of the Spaz Cola team pulled into the lead. Everyone in the crowd went wild — everyone except Wendy and Derek.

Joey was nowhere in sight.

"Are you kiddin' me?!" Derek exclaimed as the riders blazed across the finish line.

"Where's Joey?" asked Wendy.

"Not in first place, that's for sure," said Derek.

"Do you think something happened?"

"Yeah, I'm sure that fast-food eating bum ran out of steam," Derek said. "Probably collapsed in a pool of his own sweat —" Noticing Wendy's uneasiness, Derek stopped. He bit his lip and then gave her a crooked smile. "I'm sure he's fine."

Derek wrapped his arm around Wendy. The rain was still coming down hard — troubling conditions for even the best rider. Derek looked up to toward the mountain, squinting at the peak. He began to feel a little uneasy himself.

* * *

Back on Slick Rock Mountain, Joey had reached a fork in the trail. He stopped again to check the GPS. Then suddenly, he heard what sounded like several sets of footsteps coming from his left about a hundred yards away. Even though the falling rain made hearing difficult, Joey knew the footfalls weren't from an animal. They were human.

The Collective, Joey thought. *They're moving faster than I thought. There has to be a way to slow them down.*

A cawing from above caught Joey's attention. He looked into the air.

High above, a brownish-red bird landed on the branch of a young pine tree. It turned, glared at Joey, and let out a tremendous *squawk*.

Joey smiled. "A rail," he whispered to himself. "That's a King Rail."

The bird was Joey's namesake. And, although he'd been told they weren't native to the Southwest, Joey had seen one before. Actually, more than once. Whenever Joey found himself in a difficult situation, the bird would suddenly appear, and somehow Joey would find the solution to his problem.

Joey knew what he needed to do. He reached into his utility belt, pulled out his knife, and waited . . .

7

Five members of the Collective made their way up the Slick Rock Mountain and toward the Fragment's location. They moved fast, sloshing through the mud in combat boots. High-tech uniforms covered their bodies, and black helmets protected their identities.

Each of the teens wielded a defensive weapon: three of them held tranquilizer dart guns, one had a capture-net launcher, and the last carried a taser baton and the team's communication devices.

"I'm tired of tromping through this forest," said one boy with a tranquilizer. "How close are we?"

The team's radio operator pulled a GPS tracker from his belt. A high-pitched beeping echoed from the machine — one beep every three to four seconds.

"We're within an hour's walk of the Fragment," answered the radio operator.

"You've got to be kidding me!" shouted the young man with the net launcher. "We've already been hiking for half a day."

"Shut it!" commanded the group's leader. "We have a job to do. And until it's finished — until that Fragment is secured for the Old Man — I don't want to hear another word!"

"At least that Revolution punk is out of the way," added the radio operator. "It should be smooth sailing from this point forward."

The team member with the tranquilizer gun let out a "Hoorah" and continued forward down the trail. *Snap!* He stepped on a small twig. Suddenly, on the path, a green cord tightened and locked around the teen's ankle. A booby-trap! A nanosecond later, the young man was flying through the air — yanked into the sky from the force of a bent tree limb.

Instinctively, the teen pulled the trigger of his tranquilizer gun. A dart flew silently through the sky until — *thud!* — it struck another guard square in the chest. "Ugh," he said. He tried to scream out, but quickly dropped to the ground. He was completely unconscious.

The shooter dangled from a nearby tree, knocked out as well. Below him, the three other teens looked on, dumbstruck by the events. In less than five seconds, two of their team members were taken out.

Finally, the radio operator spoke. "W-what the heck just happened?!" he shouted. The teen nervously grabbed his baton off his leg, sparked it on, and then waved it back and forth through the air, searching for an invisible enemy.

Dropping to a knee, their leader held up a fist, signaling for the group to stop. Then, waving an open palm to the ground, he ordered his remaining troops into crouching positions. From the safety of some large rocks, the leader detached a high-tech cord from the sight on his weapon, wiped the rain off a small plug on one end, and then gently pushed the plug into a portal on the side of his helmet.

Click! The military-grade microcomputer inside the leader's helmet suddenly whirred to life. From inside his face shield, a small display overlaid the shooter's plastic protective mask with a video screen. The forest suddenly turned black and white. A thermal image of the area was now being broadcast to the leader's helmet directly from the scope on his weapon.

"Follow me," the leader commanded.

Slowly, the group's leader swept the area with the scope of his weapon. He searched high and low, looking for any heat signatures that might match the motion and shape of a human being.

Just then, near the edge of the cliff, a white shape shifted against the blackness of the cold landscape.

Without hesitation, the leader rose quickly and fired.

Pop! Sailing through the air, the dart zipped toward its intended target. In a second, it stuck hard into a tree, embedding itself deep in the bark.

Standing right beside the dart was Joey Rail. It had missed his neck by mere inches. Joey's booby-trap had worked — well, almost. The parachute cord had taken out two members of the Collective, but now he stood face to face with three other enemies.

"It's another one of those Revolution kids!" shouted the Collective leader, spotting Joey through the cover of some underbrush. He started running toward the boy at full sprint.

"Wait, sir!" shouted the radio officer. "What about them?" The teen pointed at his unconscious team members. One still dangled high in a tree, and the other lay on a nearby path.

"Forget those failures!" ordered the leader. "We have to complete the mission. Follow me!"

Joey hadn't counted on the Collective members actually catching up to him. He hoped his clever booby-trap would have slowed them long enough for him to reach the summit, retrieve the Fragment, and escape.

Hope is a lot like luck, Joey thought. *Never count on it.*

As Joey pedaled around trees and over rocks, the Collective members chased him on foot. They fired darts and nets at him with near accuracy.

Joey glanced over his shoulder. Through the pouring rain, he couldn't see his pursuers, but he knew they were there. *If I can't see them*, thought Joey as a dart nearly struck his arm. *How can they see me?*

Just then, Joey spotted a glowing red light behind him. *Their helmets*, he thought. *They must be equipped with some kind of high-tech sensors, like the ones Dad uses in Afghanistan!*

Whoooosh! Another dart skimmed his arm. Joey poured on the speed, hurdling obstacles of dead trees and fallen logs. But ahead of him, Joey could hear the sound of rushing water. He knew there was only a matter of seconds before he ran out of road. The cliff's edge was looming and coming up fast. Massive trees with gnarled roots protruded from the face of the cliff, and below them, a monstrous thousand-foot drop to the roaring river.

Joey knew that this spot was popular among visitors to the park. He also knew a favorite attraction lay just ahead: a wooden tower with a zip line that led to the other side of the chasm. He could grab the handle and zip line to safety on the other side of the river, but Joey knew if he took this way out — the safe route — he was certainly giving up on Omar's quest. He would have no time to double back to the Fragment before the remaining members of the Collective reached it.

As the Collective members neared, Joey considered his options: take the easy way out, or do the right thing.

8

Meanwhile, at the bottom of the mountain, the race had ended. Teams had gathered their equipment and taken their places on the winner's podium. The trophy ceremony was about to begin.

"Mr. Stevenson?!" shouted Derek. He pushed through the gathering crowd, trying to get the attention of the race sponsor.

"What's the matter?" asked the man. "I'm about to hand out the prize money —"

"It's Joey," interrupted Wendy. "He didn't come back. He should've been here by now!"

Stevenson stood silently for a moment, and then looked up at Slick Rock Mountain through the falling rain. "What route did he take?" he finally asked.

"When I last saw him, he was headed up the staircase cliffs," Derek replied. "I'm guessing Joey took that to the summit and then started down the backside."

Stevenson eyes narrowed as his thin lips turned into a crooked smile. "Clever lad," he said softly.

"Sir?" Derek asked, puzzled.

"Nothing, my boy! Nothing!" Stevenson exclaimed. Then he turned toward the racing team on the podium and waved toward the captain. "Rick!"

A tall, muscular teen quickly ran to his boss's side.

"Yes, sir?" asked Rick, standing at attention.

"Suit up again, son," ordered Stevenson. "We might have a problem on the mountain."

* * *

High above on the mountain, the three remaining Collective members reached the zip line tower at the edge of the cliff. They stopped and moved silently, covering one another with their tranquilizer guns and checking the wooden structure.

The door to the tower had been wrenched open, and the zip handle was on the other side of the three-hundred-foot chasm.

Joey was nowhere to be seen.

"He flew the coop!" shouted one of the boys.

Just then, a stirring in the underbrush nearby caught the attention of team leader. He held up a fist, the teens froze in their tracks. The leader spun with his weapon held to his shoulder and fired again.

Pop! A tranquilizer dart blasted from his rifle and struck its target.

A massive black shape leaped from the underbrush and rushed straight for the Collective members. The beast stammered, grunted, and fell to the rocky ground as the tranquilizer took hold.

It wasn't human. And, more importantly, it wasn't Joey Rail.

"What is it?" asked one of the teens.

"A wild boar!" shouted another teen gleefully.

"Nice shot," said the third member, "but that's not the *pig* we're lookin' for."

"I'm not taking any chances," replied the shooter. "That kid's already taken out two of our guys. Now, come on. We've got a mission to complete."

"You want me to call this in?" the radio operator asked, placing a hand to the button on his helmet.

The leader moved toward him and grabbed his wrist. "Are you outta your mind?" he shouted. "You want the Old Man to find out about this?"

"Of course not," the radio operator said softly.

"Then think before you act!" said the leader.

"But what about the kid?" the third guy asked. "He's still out there somewhere."

The leader nodded toward the other side of the chasm. "Forget about him," he said. "He turned chicken and ran. Now let's get moving. Double-time!"

The trio began to move.

Joey pressed a foot into the rock wall and watched as the teens headed farther down the trail. He quietly peeked over the lip of the cliff side. Trailing off into the deep recesses of the forest, the Collective members disappeared.

Joey Rail pulled himself back onto the main trail and took off running in the opposite direction. Silently, he angled his footfalls so they wouldn't make a sound. He mashed through puddles and pools of wet mud. Careful not to leave a trail, he bent tree limbs back, not breaking them, leaving no trace of his route.

They couldn't see me, he thought. *The mud! It must be camouflaging me from their sensors.*

Joey hopped on his bike. He zagged right and headed deeper in the forest, away from the cliffs, the rushing river, and the jagged rocks below.

9

Near the base of the cliff, Joey came to a path that led up the north side of the mountain. He knew the Collective members would be heading up the eastern slope. He also knew the trails on that side would be completely washed out by rain. They'd be running through thick, gooey mud the whole way — giving Joey a distinct advantage.

Even so, Joey didn't let up. He pedaled the path as quickly as he could. Smiling to himself, Joey couldn't help but wonder what his father would think of all this. Bad guys, ancient artifacts, supernatural powers, a global conspiracy . . . it all seemed so ridiculous, but wickedly exciting at the same time.

A real challenge, Joey thought.

For as long as Joey could remember, he'd wanted to be a part of something bigger than himself, something much more challenging. Most of the kids Joey grew up with wanted to ride BMX because the sport was daring, and it often made their parents mad.

Joey was different.

He had never fought with his parents and felt no need to rebel. In fact, he genuinely liked his mom and dad. They were good people. Sure, they made him do chores, finish his homework, and follow a curfew, but as long as he respected those rules, they respected him.

Then, when Joey's father was sent on his first deployment to Iraq, things changed. Suddenly, Joey found himself with all sorts of responsibilities young kids didn't normally have. Doing what he could to be "the man of the house" while his father was away, Joey missed out on being a normal kid. He grew up faster than his friends.

Within five months of his father's departure, however, Joey's mother knew her son needed something that was uniquely his own. He needed something to blow off steam and escape his added pressures. That's when she bought Joey his first BMX bike. And, before long, her son was making a name for himself in the preteen and teen freestyle circuits.

All of the outdoor activities, the woodsman training with his dad, the camping, and hiking gave him an advantage over the other competitors. He had learned discipline, work ethics, and physical endurance.

Soon, Joey received an invitation to ride in his first Spaz Cola amateur qualifier, and he beat the pants off the local competition.

With that, Joey was a local celebrity.

The world's top amateur BMX athletes were going to Salt Lake City for the finals, and Joey was invited.

The amateur series of the National Pro Tour, the event consisted of forty-seven regional events, featuring every action sport — from BMX to skateboarding. They were to be put through the ringer in their different disciplines with verts, street, park and dirt tricks and racing.

Winners from all forty-seven stops battled it out in the finals. One champion in each discipline earned a spot to compete with the pros in Las Vegas.

That day, the relative newcomer, Joey Rail, came in at second place. He didn't get to go to Vegas, but suddenly, the invitations to other events started coming and so did the sponsors. They came out of everywhere, wanting him to sign with them and promote their products.

The problem was, Joey wanted to go to college and most of the professional BMX riders were in the sport for life. Joey didn't see this as a lifestyle, but a means to an end. He wanted to get an education and make a difference to the world — like his mom and dad did.

Back on the mountain, Joey considered his the events of the day. Omar. The Revolution. It was like something out of a blockbuster movie. Not sure if Omar was in his right mind, Joey had to trust his gut. After all, the kid was the captain of the Revolution.

The Revolution, Joey thought, *that's just the kind of team I've wanted to join!* He didn't dare wonder if they'd have him as a member, but perhaps if he succeeded in this task, they'd consider it.

Joey took Omar's GPS device from his belt and checked the screen. Only 100 yards to go now, but even if he got the Fragment, would he be able to get down the mountain before the others could stop him?

10

Pacing back and forth, Derek began to actually get nervous. Had he built the bike correctly? Would his mods hold up to the stresses of the course? If something happened to Joey because of his tinkering, he'd never be able to forgive himself.

He watched as Mr. Stevenson ordered people about. "There's never been a downed rider at one of my races before, and we're not going to start now!" Stevenson yelled as the rescue teams sprang into action.

Men jumped into jeeps with medic gear as engines fired up, spitting black smoke into the air.

"What can I do, Mr. Stevenson?" Derek asked. He watched the jeep drive up the far access road toward the mountain.

"Nothing right now." Stevenson said, placing a hand on Derek's shoulder. "I'm sure we'll find him okay, right, Rick?" he said, turning to his team captain.

Snapping a plastic buckle into its holder, Rick clicked a massive utility belt with a number of pockets and pouches around his waist. "Yes, sir," Rick answered back, pulling on a pair of leather motocross gloves.

Walking over to a motocross bike, Rick strapped on a helmet that completely covered his face. He smashed his heel down on the starter and twisted the throttle. In a flash, the knobby rear tire was spitting mud up behind it. Then, finally grabbing the terrain, the motocross bike shot off like a rocket.

"Rick'll get it done, don't worry," Stevenson said as Wendy walked up behind them. "He's my number-one guy."

Slapping Derek on the back, Stevenson walked away, but Wendy, completely perplexed, stood and stared as Rick rode off. "Where's he going?" she asked.

"After Joey," Derek snapped. "Where else would he be headed?"

"Not that way he isn't," Wendy said. She pulled her map from her pocket and laid it on the hood of a truck. "According to Joey, he was going to traverse the mountain *here*."

Wendy pointed to Joey's original route that took him off the beaten path and toward the top slope.

Derek scratched his head. "So?" he said.

"Joey didn't go up Slick Rock Mountain, he went up Devil's Peak," she exclaimed.

"Then why the heck is Rick heading over to Slick Rock Mountain?" asked Derek suspiciously.

* * *

By midday, the sun still couldn't cut through the dense, overcast blanket of gray clouds. That was fine with the three members of the Collective who trekked along the steep mountain fire access road toward the top of Slick Rock Mountain.

The crisp air kept them cool in their thick, black suits of leather and Kevlar as they made their way to the northern side of the summit.

"I'm getting a reading on the locater!" the radio operator said excitedly. The GSP tracker beeped quickly and loudly in his hands.

The second in command sighed loudly. "It's about time," he said. "How much farther?"

"Two hundred yards to the end zone," the radio operator exclaimed.

"Thank God," the group's leader replied. "I just want to go home and get some sleep."

"Shut up!" the radio operator ordered, placing a hand to the receiver on his ear.

"Don't tell me to shut up!" the leader said.

"Quiet!" repeated the teen. "It's the Old Man!"

Without another word, the group's leader shut his mouth. Though the two other teens couldn't hear what the radio operator was saying, they knew it had to be important. The Old Man never contacted them unless it was urgent.

Finally, the radio operator lowered his hand from his ear. "The Old Man knows about the other kid," he reported. "He says not to engage."

"Why?" questioned the leader.

"They're sending a specialist to deal with him," replied the radio operator. "Our mission's the Fragment."

Throwing his hands in the air, the leader gave up. "Whatever," he said. "I get paid either way, so let's go."

The other members followed his lead, continuing on their path to the summit.

*   *   *

Joey had reached the summit of Slick Rock
Mountain. The area was about 50 yards square, in a
diamond shape. The flat crag on the right was the drop,
and the men would be coming from the east.

Joey knew this area better than his own backyard.
The south-facing rock face of the mountain was a
sheer drop to the riverbed below. Scattered trees and
outcropping rock formations littered the summit, but
for the most part, it was barren.

Deep crags and crevasses were filled with water, but
they could trap a man if he weren't careful. Joey needed
to watch where he stepped.

Glancing back and forth from the GPS device to the
plateau, Joey began his search for the Fragment. Omar
had told him it would probably be encrusted with mud,
about a good three feet below the surface.

Riding back and forth, Joey waited for the GPS
locator to lock in on the piece until finally —

WELCOME TO THE REVOLUTION RAIL

11

Joey shoved the Fragment into his pocket. He
quickly scooped up handfuls of mud and began
spreading it all over his face and body.

Coming over the ridgeline, the three members of the
Collective moved with the precision of a well-trained
military unit. Throwing hand signals like deranged
third-base coaches allowed them to move without
speaking to one another.

The group's leader used his thermal scope to scan
for any signs of organic life. Nothing registered. The
other teens moved slowly, surveying the scene.

Large boulders, some trees, massive puddles
of water and low bushes filled the area just below the
summit as they began to move into the area.

The radio operator stood still as the other two spread out, moving even more slowly.

Beep! Beep! The tracking device squealed. "We're right on top of it!" the radio operator announced. "Three meters east and one north!"

As the group's leader stepped up, he didn't see the small amount of latticework below his feet, thanks to the tree limbs and leaves placed over it.

The camouflaged trap door gave way, and the teens fell straight into a massive crevasse. Up to his neck in thick, glue-like mud and water, the leader screamed for help. "Get me outta here!" he ordered.

The third teen approached and knelt on the ground. Placing his weapon on the ground, he reached over and clasped hands with his commander. "Don't worry," he assured the leader.

But at that instant, the bush next to him came alive. Looking up, the teen could hardly believe his eyes as a man-shaped bush rocketed right at him.

From the lip of the ridgeline, the radio operator screamed. Having used his knife to make small holes in his leathers, Joey Rail had plunged pieces of dead trees, bush limbs, and fallen leaves all over his clothing, camouflaging himself against the natural background.

Caked on in layers, the thick, cool mud had shielded him from their sensors, allowing Joey to hide and wait for just the right moment to strike.

"It's the kid!" shouted the radio operator. He leveled his capture-net gun and fired.

Poom! With blast of smoke, the net launched from the end of the rifle and soared right for Joey.

Joey quickly dodged the incoming net. It flew by him, but managed to hit the other squad member square in the chest. The bolo balls wrapped around him several times, and he dropped to the ground, swaddled up like a massive burrito.

"You idiot!" the teen soldier yelled as he writhed on the ground.

Joey vaulted past the third man. As he ran, he grabbed the baton off the other's leg, sparking it on. Twirling it in his hands like a baseball bat, Joey turned his attention to the radio operator, sprinting right for him.

The operator hurried to reload the capture gun. With a new net in the cartridge, he pulled the bolt back and prepared to fire.

12

Joey swung the baton through the air and smashed it down on the soldier's shoulder.

Sparks flew as the taser baton contacted the wet, leather surface of the operator's uniform. In a small convulsive fit, he shook into unconsciousness.

Turning around, Joey quickly walked back to the two other men. "Sleep tight," Joey said, tasering the net-bound soldier.

"And you!" Joey pointed the baton right at the man trapped in the mud. "Stop squirming! As soon as it stops raining, the mud will thicken up, and you'll be able to climb out."

"When will that be?!" the leader asked.

"Forecast said rain for the next three days," Joey said with a smirk.

"Three days?!" the teen squealed.

"Nighty-night," Joey said as he gently tapped the leader on the shoulder with his baton. The soldier was out like a light.

Joey wiped the mud from his face as the sound of feet crunching on rocks behind him drew his attention.

"Not bad, kid," a voice boomed out behind him.

Turning around, Joey's eyes narrowed as he viewed the figure in front of him. "Rick?" Joey asked.

Reaching up, the man removed his helmet and dropped it on the ground. Smiling from ear to ear, Rick Jackson stood, a taser baton in his right hand.

It wasn't the fact that Rick was a member of the Collective that gave Joey a shock. It was the small amount of red electricity that was flowing from one of the pouches on Rick's belt that alarmed him.

"The Fragment?" Joey asked, nodding toward the belt.

Raising an eyebrow, Rick said nothing. His calm demeanor was shaken a bit by Joey's comment, but Rick stood fast.

"So that must make Mr. Stevenson —" Joey began.

"If you want to live through the rest of this day, I'd shut that hole in your face and forget you ever heard that name," Rick threatened, his voice smooth and low.

Joey stood quietly as Rick cocked his head to the side.

Reaching out his left hand, Rick turned his palm up, fingers open. "Give it to me," he commanded.

Joey grinned. "Why?" he asked.

"Think about what we can do for you," Rick replied. "The power, brother. Look, man, we're both riders. We both know what it's like to rip through the mud, feel the ground drop away from beneath our feet and soar through the air. With what you have, and our training, you could become the best rider ever. Riches, man, like you've never imagined will be yours. And the ladies?" Rick whistled.

Joey nodded. "Sounds nice," he said.

"Nice? That's nothin', man. It's just the beginning! When the Revolution comes, you're gonna be happy you're on the right side," said Rick.

"And the rest of the planet?" Joey asked.

"They either get on board and follow us, or they get left behind," said Rick.

Joey pulled pieces of camouflage away from his hair and body.

"Well, it is tempting," Joey replied. "Especially the part about the girls."

"So what do you say?" Rick asked, stretching out his hand again.

"You must not know me," Joey said.

"Actually, I know you pretty well, Rail."

"Then you know my answer," Joey said.

Rick frowned. "You gonna stand by that?"

Joey nodded.

"No chance you'd change your mind?" asked Rick.

Joey shook his head and slowly tightened his grip on the baton in his hand. He only had an instant to react as Rick covered the ground between them in a heartbeat.

Coming down hard, Rick slammed his baton over-handed toward Joey's head.

Managing to put up his baton just in time, Joey blocked the blow, and jumped out of the way.

They squared off, sizing each other up as they circled one another. Joey's assumption was that the power of the artifact was making Rick faster, giving him extra strength and making him more agile.

He hoped the fragment in his pocket would do the same for him!

Joey came in fast, swinging at Rick's shoulder, but Rick was able to parry the slice with ease.

Joey swung the baton with speed and force, but each time he did, Rick was able to block the attack.

Exchanging blows, the batons clashed, sending electric sparks across the sky!

The falling rain made the ground soft and unsure. It was obvious to Joey that Rick was a more competent combatant. He knew Rick had done this type of thing before.

"Dude, come on," Rick said as he easily parried another swoosh and lunged forward.

Jumping back quickly, Joey panted for breath. He held up his baton, protecting himself.

"If we're gonna do this, at least try and make it look like you wanna win?" Rick said mockingly.

With a fresh grip on his baton, Joey took a second and centered himself. His breathing steadied, his nerves calmed, and suddenly, a small amount of blue electricity began to flow from the object in his pocket. It crept up over his shoulder and down into his hands. Joey Rail was renewed.

Rick smiled. "Aw yeah! That's it, Joey. Bring it!" the teen said, laughing maniacally. He waved Joey toward him. "Come at me, bro!"

Raising his baton in the air, Joey went at Rick again, but this time, his blows were more intense.

The strikes were faster, harder. With each swing of the baton, Joey found he was actually driving Rick back.

"Not bad, kid!" said Rick. The teen upped the tempo of his attacks. "But not good enough!"

Baton swirling in the air, Joey swung and parried Rick's incoming blows, but it became too much for him. One slam after another, Rick crashed down on Joey's blocks, hammering away at him.

Joey couldn't fight back. Pushed to his absolute limit, he dropped to a knee as his left leg slipped from under him.

Rick raised his boot and came down hard on Joey's chest, kicking him into the mud. The force of the blow sent Joey stumbling and sliding backwards, heading straight for the cliff's edge.

Turning on his stomach, Joey dropped his baton and desperately reached out, grasping at anything he could to slow his slide toward the edge of the bluff.

As he slipped and slid toward certain death, Joey managed to luckily grab hold of a tree limb with his left hand, stopping his slide. Face down and gazing right over the cliff, Joey's eyes popped out of his head as he realized how close he'd come to falling off.

Behind him, he heard Rick slowly approaching.

"I told the Old Man you wouldn't join us," Rick said. He reached down and picked up Joey's weapon.

Cocking his arm back, he tossed Joey's baton over the edge of the cliff. End over end, the taser tumbled down the three-hundred-foot drop toward the rough waters below. It finally disappeared into the white caps of the rapids.

Turning over, Joey got up on his elbows and scowled. "Just do it already," he grunted.

Rick smiled. He raised the baton over his head, and said, "With pleasure."

At that moment, a strange look crawled across Rick's face. He lowered his arm, seemingly very confused. Slowly, his eyes rolled into the back of his head. His knees buckled. Then, his body crumpled collapsed onto the ground.

Joey climbed to his elbows. Sticking out of Rick's back was a five-inch long silver tube with a red-feathered tail on its end.

A tranquilizer dart.

Just beyond, on the far end of the cliff, stood Derek. He held a smoking tranquilizer rifle that was tucked tightly into his shoulder.

Derek lowered the rifle as Wendy ran up behind him.

"Nice shot!" Wendy exclaimed. She ran past him and over to Joey's side.

"Yeah, not too shabby," Derek said quietly. His eyes were wide in amazement that he had actually made the shot.

Crouching down, Wendy took hold of Joey's hand and helped him to his feet.

Joey stood, looking down at Rick's unconscious body. "You okay?" Wendy asked.

"I am now," Joey said. "How did you know where I was?"

"Easy," Derek said, turning and reaching out a helping hand toward a figure behind him. Grabbing it, the familiar figure made his way up the mountainside. He hobbled up the path, holding a padded metal crutch under his arm.

Joey smiled. "Omar Grebs," he said. Looks like you found them."

"And it's a good thing for you!" Omar shot back, pointing at the fallen figure.

Joey walked over to join the others. He pointed over to Rick's unconscious body, lying face down in the mud. "Who, this guy?" Joey said, grinning. "I had it covered the entire time."

Looking past them, Joey could see Rick's motocross cycle about a hundred feet down the mountain. Parked next to it on the fire access road was Derek's truck.

Good thing they have all-weather mud tires! Joey thought to himself.

Looking around at the gaggle of unconscious Collective members, Omar chuckled. "Yeah, maybe you did have it covered," he admitted.

"Stevenson!" Joey said, suddenly remembering.

"Gone," Derek said. "He took off right after Rick came up here. We followed him and picked up your friend on the way."

"But he's the Old Man!" Joey exclaimed.

Eyes narrowing, Omar looked at Wendy and Derek, and then back to Joey as if to say, unsure if they could be trusted.

"They're coo," said Joey. "You can trust them. So what're you going to do to the Old Man? Arrest him?"

"Arrest him?" Derek asked. "For what?"

"We let him go," said Omar. "Sure, we can catch one of the big cats, but then the entire pride gets away. No, we play this one out. We've had suspicions, but now we have facts. As far as we know, Stevenson's actually a low-level operative in the Collective."

"The Collective? Wait — what's going on?!" Derek said, exasperated.

"I'll tell you later," Omar said, slapping him on the back. "It's a heck of a story."

They all headed down toward the truck together, smiling and laughing.

13

Later that afternoon, Joey stood next to Omar while in the hospital's emergency room. Omar was having his ankle professionally wrapped by Joey's mother, Joanna.

"Sounds like quite the story," Joey's mother said. She only half-believed the story, but she knew her son wasn't the type to make up stories like that, so there had to be truth in it somewhere.

"Ma'am," Omar said as he looked at her. "I promise you, everything Joey has just told you is completely true. If it weren't for him, I'd be dead and the Fragment would now be in the hands of the Collective."

"And just where is this 'Fragment,' anyway?" she asked.

Static electricity built up in Joey's hand as he reached into his pocket and pulled the mud-covered Fragment from his jacket. Walking over to the sink, he turned the tap to a trickle and ran the small object under the water.

Slowly, the mud and stones began to fall away as Joey rolled it around in the stream of hot water. Finally, the Fragment was revealed to be a small piece of composite rubber.

He shook the excess water from its surface and turned around, holding it up in the air for the others to see.

"It's just part of a broken skateboard wheel," Joanna said, still not convinced.

Joey closed his eyes and concentrated. He closed his hands over the small ball gently. From between his fingers, the blue electricity burst out, organically flowing over his hands and filling the dimly lit room with a cobalt-colored glow.

Joanna's eyes went wide. She was shocked at what was happening right in front of her eyes. Joey's body was engulfed in a field of soft, blue energy.

"That's — that's impossible," she said softly. But at that moment, she knew that everything Joey had told her was true.

Joey walked over to Omar. He held the Fragment out for him to take.

"I think this belongs to you, " said Joey as he offered it to him.

Omar opened his palm. Joey gently dropped the item into Omar's open, relaxed hand.

As soon as it left contact with Joey's skin, however, the electrical field stopped arcing. Confused, Joey glanced from the fragment to Omar, then back again.

Looking up at Joey, Omar smiled. He handed it back to Joey. "Actually," Omar said, "I think it belongs to you."

Joey took the small ball into his hands. He felt a warm sensation course through his body as the Fragment began to glow. It filled him with strength, confidence, and bravery. With that energy flowing over him, Joey felt like there wasn't anything he couldn't accomplish.

For the first time in his life, Joey had found what he had been searching for — a team. A place where he mattered. Where he knew he'd be able to make a difference.

Omar could tell exactly how Joey felt. He, too, had sensed the very same feeling not that long ago when he had gone on a similar personal journey.

Omar offered his hand to Joey. Joey shook hands with his new brother-in-arms.

"Welcome to the Revolution, Joey Rail." Omar said.

JOEY RAIL_
CODE NAME: RAIL

AGE: 14

HOMETOWN: Moab, Utah

SPORT: BMX Freestyle

INTERESTS: Animal Rights, Environmental Activism, Outdoors

BIO: Growing up in Moab, fourteen-year-old Joey Rail learned to ride before he could walk. He's tried every two-wheeled sport imaginable (motocross, mountain biking, etc.), but he's always come back to BMX freestyle. The skill, patience, and power required for this daring sport suit his personality. Joey is an outdoor enthusiast and loves taking things to the edge. On days that he's not competing, he's skinning his knees on the red stone of Slickrock Trail, cliff jumping off the banks of Lake Powell, or rafting down the Red River. You'll never find him wearing anything other than jeans and a t-shirt — except, of course, on a moonlit training ride. On those nights, he'll throw on a dusty flannel to protect again the cool desert winds.

STORY SETTING: Desert

LOCATING...

ABOUT TONY HAWK

TONY HAWK is the most famous and influential skateboarder of all time. In the 1980s and 1990s, he was instrumental in skateboarding's transformation from fringe pursuit to respected sport. After retiring from competitions in 2000, Tony continues to skate demos and tour all over the world.

He is the founder, President, and CEO of Tony Hawk Inc., which he continues to develop and grow. He is also the founder of the Tony Hawk Foundation, which works to create skateparks and empower youth in low income communities.

TONY HAWK WAS THE FIRST SKATEBOARDER TO LAND THE 900 TRICK, A 2.5 REVOLUTION (900 DEGREES) AERIAL SPIN, PERFORMED ON A SKATEBOARD RAMP.

ABOUT THE AUTHOR_

M. ZACHARY SHERMAN is a veteran of the United States Marine Corps. He has written comics for Marvel, Radical, Image, and Dark Horse. His recent work includes *America's Army: The Graphic Novel*, *Earp: Saint for Sinners*, and the second book in the *SOCOM: SEAL Team Seven* trilogy.

ABOUT Q & A_

Q: WHEN DID YOU DECIDE TO BECOME A WRITER?

A: I've been writing all my life, but the first professional gig I ever had was a screenplay for Illya Salkind (*Superman 1–3*) back in 1995. But it was a secondary profession, with small assignments here and there, and it wasn't until around 2005 that I began to get serious.

Q: HAS YOUR MILITARY EXPERIENCE AFFECTED YOUR WRITING?

A: Absolutely, especially the discipline I have obtained. Time management is key when working on projects, so you must be able to govern yourself. In regards to story, I've met and been with many different people, which enabled me to become a better storyteller through character.

Q: WHAT OTHER PROJECTS HAVE YOU WORKED ON?

A: I've written several comic projects for companies like Marvel Comics and Image Comics, but I've also written screenplays for several movie projects that are this close to being made into films. And of course, video games like *SAW, Rogue Warrior,* and *America's Army*.

TONY HAWK'S 900 revolution

TONY HAWK'S 900 REVOLUTION, VOL. 1: DROP IN

Omar Grebes never slows down. When he's not shredding concrete at Ocean Beach Skate Park, he's kicking through surf or scarfing down fish tacos from the nearest roadside shop. Soon, his live-or-die lifestyle catches the attention of big-name sponsors. But one of them offers Omar more than he bargained for . . . a chance to become the first member of the mysterious 900 Revolution team and claim his piece of history.

TONY HAWK'S 900 REVOLUTION, VOL. 2: IMPULSE

When you skate in New York, it's all about getting creative, and fourteen-year-old Dylan Crow considers himself a street artist. You won't catch him tagging alley walls. Instead, he paints the streets with his board. He wants to be seen grinding rails in Brooklyn and popping ollies at the Chelsea Piers. But when Dylan starts running with the wrong crowd, his future becomes a lot less certain . . . until he discovers the Revolution.

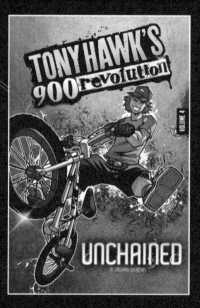

TONY HAWK'S 900 REVOLUTION, VOL. 3: FALL LINE

Amy Kestrel is a powder pig. Often hidden beneath five layers of hoodies, this bleach-blonde, CO ski bum is tough to spot on the street. However, get her on the slopes, and she's hard to miss. Amy always has the latest and greatest gear. But when a group of masked men threaten her mountain, she'll need every ounce of the one thing she lacks — confidence — and only the Revolution can help her find it.

TONY HAWK'S 900 REVOLUTION, VOL. 4: UNCHAINED

Joey Rail learned to ride before he could walk. He's tried every two-wheeled sport imaginable, but he's always come back to BMX freestyle. The skills required for this daring sport suit his personality. Joey is an outdoor enthusiast and loves taking risks. But when he's approached by the first three members of the Revolution, Joey must make a decision . . . follow the same old path or take the road less traveled.

As Dylan Crow neared the flat bar, he kicked his
board up and did 5-0 grind across its length. Amy
Kestrel knew that was a deliberate trick. Difficult, yet
done with such casualness that it told the other skaters
to make room. They were going to be schooled.

Dylan headed straight for the nearest ramp to get
some elevation. At its top, he spun a 360 and then
headed toward the nearest rail. He kick-flipped his
board up, did a grind across the rail, and then flipped
his board again as he reached the end of the rail,
landing the trick perfectly.

He may be an arrogant showoff, but he was good.
Amy had to admit that. She just hoped nobody noticed
the trace of blue electricity that followed Dylan's
skateboard from trick to trick.

Dylan ran through a few other tricks. Some Amy
couldn't even name. As skaters gathered to watch, he
did a nose stall at the top of a ramp to check out the
crowd. This was his moment. Dylan had their attention.

Amy felt a brush on her shoulder, almost like the
flutter of wings.

"Is that your friend," a voice whispered in her ear.

Amy turned to see a pixie-ish girl with spiked red hair and tube-sock arm bands.

"Um, yeah," Amy replied, distracted.

Just then, the crowd of skaters hooted and hollered. Amy turned, but Dylan had all ready landed his trick. *Dang, I missed it*, she muttered to herself.

"So what do you want?" she turned back toward the girl, sounding more annoyed then she meant to.

"I- I-," the girl stammered. "He's pretty good. Does he ride for anyone?"

Amy should have known it. Another groupie falling for the good-looking, arrogant showoff.

"Yeah, he's with a team. We both are."

"Really? You, too?"

"Yeah, though I'm more into powder than pavement."

Just then, Dylan skated up to them, all sweaty and out of breath.

"Who's your friend?" he asked Amy as he flashed the pixie-ish girl a smile.

"I'm Wren," she replied, more to Amy than Dylan.

Read more in the next adventure of . . .

Tony Hawk's 900 Revolution

TONY HAWK'S
900 revolution